Hetty
the hen who couldn't lay

Written by Sarah Igo

Illustrated by Rebecca Williamson

Matador
Unit E2 Airfield Business Park,
Harrison Road, Market Harborough,
Leicestershire. LE16 7UL
Tel: 0116 2792299
Email: books@troubador.co.uk
Web: www.troubador.co.uk/matador
Twitter: @matadorbooks

ISBN 978 1803131 535

British Library Cataloguing in Publication Data.
A catalogue record for this book is available from the British Library.

Printed and bound by Ashford Colour Press Ltd, Hampshire, PO13 0FW

Matador is an imprint of Troubador Publishing Ltd

For Beth and Dillon

Alone in her coop on a bedful of hay
sat Hetty, the hen who just couldn't lay.
Each night she would settle on top of her nest,
plump out her feathers and try her dear best.

Then morning would come and she'd lift up her leg,
expecting to find a beautiful egg.

Her sisters would cluck: "It'll happen you'll see."
Laying egg upon egg so naturally.

"Try eating some grit,"
one said in the yard.
And so Hetty did, crunching
down really hard.

But as evening fell,
just like all the rest,
no egg tumbled down
to fill up her nest.

"A bed of soft straw will bring you a chick,"
Wise Old Hen clucked through a mouthful of sticks.
Down Hetty settled to wait for the night,
yet woke to the same, sad empty sight.

"Just one chick for me, not a flock or a clutch.
I'd be happy you see, I don't want so much,"
Hetty confided one night as she wept
to her kind younger sister, the sweet Harriet.

As the hens settled down one by one for a sleep,
into young Harriet's head an idea came to creep.

"Psst! Hello there Hetty – are you still awake?
I've plenty of eggs, here's one you can take!"

"That's awfully kind, but what's in it for you? I can't give one back, although I'd love to."
"Dear sis, don't be silly," she said with a smile.
"Seeing you happy is all I desire."

Nudge, roll then flutter and in she did tuck
an egg beneath Hetty, wishing her luck.
Hetty beamed broadly "Oh, thank you!" she said
as kind Harriet fluttered back to her bed.

On top of her nest
sat Hetty so proudly,
"An egg at long last!"
she cried ever so loudly.
Day after day
Hetty kept her egg warm,
puffing her feathers
against the cold storm.

One day she awoke from a much sweeter sleep
and out from the egg popped her chick with a cheep!
"Hurray!" cried Harriet. "Now your chick's here!"
As all of her sisters applauded with cheers.

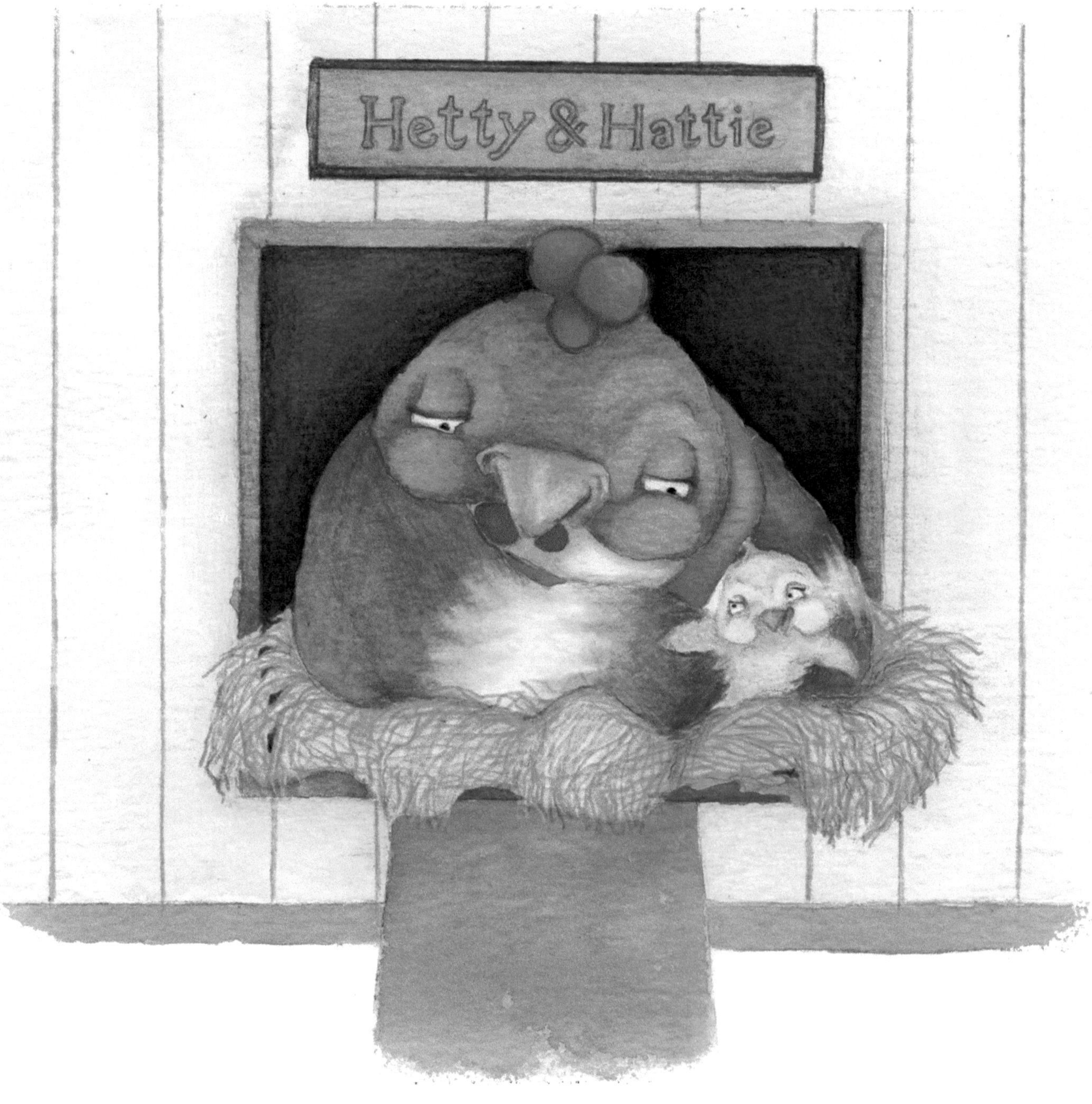
Hetty & Hattie

Hetty protected the chick with her wing.
Filled up with great joy she started to sing:
"Oh Harriet, Harriet, thank you so much.
I didn't want a brood, a litter or a clutch.
One chick, just one chick, that's all, do you see?
And no hen in the world could be happier than me."

The End

Honesty is always the best policy. Especially when it comes backed up by a cracking allegory.

At the age of 14, after a number of scans failed to find a set of ovaries, I was dutifully informed by a dour doctor that I would 'never be able to have babies'. Discharged in an era when the Internet wasn't quite the all-knowing oracle it is today and counselling wasn't even suggested, all hopes of one day having a family were dismissed.

At 34, my 20-year-old sister offered to donate her eggs, gifting me with a chance at motherhood. Nine months later, my daughter Dillon was born.

Dillon, now 3, has known from the start that 'mummy didn't have any eggs', and that 'Aba gave you some eggs'. The story attached, Hetty The Hen Who Couldn't Lay was written to honour my sister's immeasurable act of love and altruism (as Hetty says – 'what's in it for you? I can't give one back, although I'd love to') and as a gentle comparison for Dillon – who clicked immediately 'mummy Hetty didn't have any eggs just like you'.

The stunning illustrations come from Rebecca Williamson, a talented artist, illustrator, designer and friend. She breathed life into the characters in a way I could only dream of. I always intended to have this story published, in the hope that it might help other Hettys, Harriets and 'chicks'.

Thanks for reading
Sarah
www.wordsbywoodslea.com

Based in the South Lakes, I love the outdoors, and when I'm not busy illustrating, you'll most likely find me on top of a fell! I studied illustration at Leeds Arts University and I mainly specialise in portraiture, of both people and pets. I always strive to create work that evokes emotion and creates a connection, so when Sarah approached me with this story I leapt at the opportunity to be involved in creating something so important that will resonate with millions of people. It's a story that should be told, and a topic that deserves to be talked about. My aim was to create illustrations that were not only fun, colourful and appealing to children, but that would also convey the deep emotions involved in the real-life process of IVF.
I hope this story has resonated with you as much as it has with me.

Rebecca
www.rebeccawilliamsonillustration.com